The Rude,

Crude,

Lewd,

Read Aloud

Book

A Merv d'Perv Production.

The Rude, Crude, Lewd, Read Aloud Book

INTRODUCTION.

Everybody's on their mobile phones.
All the time!
We forward things that amuse us.
We read comments or jokes and forward them on to our loved ones so they can do the same.
We forward links to funny/sad/old video clips to friends who we know (or hope) will appreciate them.
But we don't get to see how they react!

We don't know if they liked them or laughed at them, or indeed, if they even watched them!

In days gone by, people told jokes or funny stories, or recited funny rhymes to each other and most of the time, the teller of the story got as much enjoyment from the telling of them as the listener got from the listening to them.

Also, if the joke or story was good enough, the listeners would tell it to other people.

And so on.

Perhaps it's time we brought that back!

"The Rude, Crude, Lewd, Read aloud book" contains over 50 poems designed to delight, disgust, disturb, educate, advise and possibly offend your audience.

The instructions are simple -

1. Pick a poem.
2. Read it out loud to someone else (you might want to practice it first).
3. **Watch their reaction!**

Merv d'Perv Productions

CONTENTS.

CONTENTS

Clear Out

I stick my finger up my nose,
I swirl it all around,
I pull it out,
And if in doubt,
I flick it on the ground.
Sometimes it's green,
Sometimes it's black,
It can be smooth or rough,
But if my finger comes out red?
I know I've poked enough!

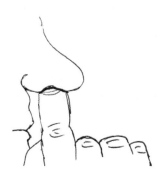

The Icing On the Cake

I was standing in the public toilets,
I was busting for a wee-wee and a shite,
I was in an awful state,
And I really couldn't wait,
So I took the closest cubicle in sight.

Then I closed the creaky door,
and I pulled my trousers down,
I was just about to open up my hole,
When I took a little glance,
Towards my underpants,
And I saw a massive shit inside the bowl.

Well my first thought it was this,
"I must postpone my poo and piss"
So I tightened up my bum and tried to stop,
But there wasn't any smell,
So I just thought "What the hell"
And I went ahead and did mine on the top!

Grounds For Divorce?

I miss you in the morning,
I miss you late at night,
It's just not fair,
I must repair,
My telescopic sight!

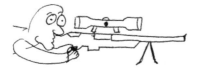

Confession

I said my love would never die,
She answered with a snigger,
She said she loved some other guy,
That's why I pulled the trigger!

Tidy Up Time 1

My gorgeous girlfriend's pubic hair,
Was shiny, long and black,
One day I looked - it wasn't there !!!
She'd shaved it,
- "For the craic"

Tidy Up Time 2

I shaved my balls, they're really bare,
My girlfriend thinks it's cool,
My balls are cold without their hair,
But you wanna see the size of my tool!

Dilemma

I walk real fast,
I walk real slow,
I slip and slide my feet,

It's hard to scratch an itchy hole,
When you're walking down the street.

A Liquid Lunch

I saw this guy the other day,
On his nose a massive drip,
And I watched with horror and dismay,
As it fell onto his lip.

His tongue came out, he tasted it,
Then he licked his lips in glee,
And I couldn't believe that Dirty Shit,
Did that in front of me.

So I put him straight,
I said "Hey mate,
It's clear that you've got issues,

So here's two poun' you dirty clown,
Go an' buy some fuckin' tissues"

Justified Impatience

I was standing in the checkout queue,
And there's nothing really worse,
Than an oul doll right in front of you
When she's hoking for her purse.

Her stuff's been all put through the till,
And I don't think it's funny,
She waits 'til now,
The dozy cow,
To get her fucking money.

Consideration

There's something that really annoys me,
There's something I really don't like,
And it's time I confessed,
That this thing I detest,
Is those fuckers out riding their bike.

With their arse in the air,
Those boys really don't care,
That the traffic behind them has slowed,
So I'd just like to say,
Hope youse have a nice day,
But please GET THE FUCK OUT OF MY ROAD!

Now they're riding in packs,
With their hairy arse cracks
On display,it's a fucking disgrace,
And it's time that they learned,
That respect must be earned,
Or else GET THE FUCK OUT OF OUR SPACE!

When I'm driving my car,
And I'm travelling far,
With insurance and road tax to pay,
All I see right in front,
Is a freeloading C#nt
So dude GET THE FUCK OUT OF MY WAY!

Live Long and Prostate!

These aliens abducted me,
About a week ago,
They stuck a pole,
Right up my hole,
And moved it to and fro.
I think they've also brainwashed me,
Cos deep inside my brain,
These same five words are on repeat,
"I hope they call again!"

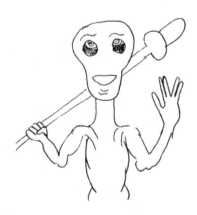

Unlucky Catch

I did a big sneeze, it was really unplanned,
And my snatters flew out like a rocket,
But I'd done it right into the palm of my hand,
So I wiped them all off in my pocket.

Simple "Number 2" Potty Training.

"Just wipe and look"

- That's all it took!

Needs Must

I was sitting on the toilet,
And I had to clean my hole,
But the paper it was finished,
So I used the cardboard roll!

Road Rage

I love to drive my little car,
I know my Highway Code,
I follow it religiously,
When driving on the road,
But other people aren't the same,
The code they have forgotten,
I think it is an awful shame,
Their driving skills are rotten.

I was driving just the other day,
When I came across this trucker,
He was driving really close to me,
The STUPID UGLY FUCKER,
His lorry was right up my ass,
(cos I was out in front),
He tried and tried but couldn't pass,
The DOPEY USELESS C##T

Well finally he got around,
So I waved to be polite,
But he stuck his middle finger up,
The IGNORANT BIG FAT SHITE.

But the firm's name it was on the back,
So he got a big surprise,
I got that ignorant pig the sack,
Cos I told them loads of lies.

And later on while driving home
I saw this stupid bitch,
She was talking on her mobile phone,
So I put her in the ditch!

Just Desserts

If you lie or cheat or steal,
Or think you have the right,
You'll meet a man who makes you squeal,
When in your cell at night!

Eight Out Of Ten

My girlfriend's little "Foo Foo" is the nicest that I've seen,
She really takes good care of it, she keeps it nice and clean,
It's always trimmed and tidy as my girlfriend's really fussy,
But that's enough about her dog – let's talk about her pussy!

Her pussy's black and hairy and it's really soft to touch,
It's always glad to see me and I like it very much,
But sometimes it smells fishy and I don't mean to be rude,
My girlfriend doesn't spend a lot, she buys it cheap catfood!

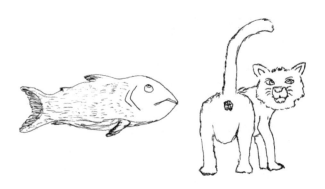

The Shopping Channel

When I come home you're always there,
You're waiting by the door,
You bring my slippers to the chair,
To you it's not a chore.

You sit and listen to my day,
On me your love is spent,
I often wonder why you stay,
You must be heaven sent.

I got you when I lost my wife,
My heart you've helped to mend,
You've made me turn around my life,
My ever faithful friend.

I still recall the day we met,
You never left my side,
The money I do not regret,
My gorgeous Asian bride!

False Economy

I've had a little accident,
My fingernail is brown,
I went and bought cheap toilet roll,
When shopping in the town.
The lesson I have learned is that
When buying toilet roll,
Never buy the cheaper brand,
It's useless on the whole!

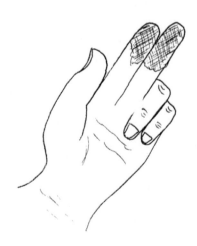

70's Throwback

Global Warming, Climate Change,
It's all a load of shite,
And you Environmentalists,
Can kiss my ass goodnight.

Recycling is a load of balls,
So shove your coloured bins,
And all you Eco-Warriors,
Can die for all my tins.

Eating meat is good for you,
It makes you big and strong,
And all you Vegetarians,
Are just plain fucking wrong.

And Politicians? Fuck Right Off
Cos no-one wants to know you,
You've only just'
Got back our trust,
(As far as we could throw you!)

And as for all this Gender crap,
Please stop your silly noise,
Cos little girls are little girls,
And boys are bloody boys!
Don't tell them what to say or do,
Or how to act or think,
(For the record, boys are dressed in blue,
And little girls in pink!)

To those of you who think I'm mad,
I say to you "That's fine
But just you live your own sweet life,
And fuck off out of mine!"

A Touch Of Class

My little dog is so polite,
He says "I beg your pardon"
When every time he does a shite,
In my next door neighbour's garden.

Dead Giveaway

I let a fart out by mistake,
I thought no-one could tell,
I thought I'd got away with it,
But then they smelt the smell!

Beside The Seaside

My gorgeous girlfriend's pubic hair,
Was black and long and shiny,
But every time she did a wee,
It tasted slightly briny!

Hop On, Hop Off

I got a boner on the bus,
An awkward situation,
I didn't think there'd be a fuss,
With public masturbation.

But one thing I now know for sure,
The public do not like it,
I can't get on the bus no more,
For me it's bike or hike it!

Checkout Operator

They stand and stare,
Without a care,
They talk about me too,
They stand and wait,
Intimidate,
I fucking hate that queue!

Strangulation

My girlfriend's sexy underwear,
It drives me up the walls,
I love her skimpy panties,
But they're too tight round my balls!

Flog My Log

My girlfriend's quite dyslexic,
I should have seen the signs,
We make love several times a day,
(She says she loves my Pines!)

Halloween 1

It's really dark,
You're all alone,
The lights are out,
You have no phone,
You hear a sound,
A sudden creak,
Your throat is dry,
You cannot speak,
There's something here,
It's nothing good,
It's something evil,
Seeking food,
The air's disturbed,
It's just passed by,
You're terrified,
You want to cry,
An awful stench,
What is that smell?
(Deep down you know,
This won't end well)

Another noise,
It sounded near,
Imagination,
Changes gear.....

Halloween 1 continued....

A Devils' face,
It grins in glee,
I can't see it,
But it sees me,
A slimy tongue,
It licks its' lips,
Saliva falls,
In little drips.
A mouth crammed full,
Of broken teeth,
(With gums the colour
of my wreath)
A white dead face,
With blood red eyes,
About to give me
My surprise......

Or maybe not,
You could be wrong,
Your brain is stringing
you along,
Vampires and ghosts,
The walking dead,
They're all inside
Your aching head.

These things aren't real,
You know that much,

Then on your cheek,
a gentle touch....!

Halloween 2

Halloween is real good fun,
If you can keep your head,
If vampires are behind you, run!
Or you could end up dead!
A shrivelled corpse all drained and dry,
No blood left in your veins,
And don't forget your mum's loud cry
Cos blood leaves awful stains

Open Sesame

My gorgeous girlfriend's pubic hair,
Is shiny, black and long,
She has to comb it to the side,
To let in "Mister Dong"

Men only – Part one

A massive shite,
A big long pee,
These things can feel,
Like ecstasy,
But where pleasure's concerned,
These things can't match,
Giving your balls,
A good old scratch!

Men only – Part two

There's nothing worse if you're a lad,
Than having to flush a fanny-pad.

Damsel In Shitdress

I was down the town the other day,
When this pretty girl passed me by,
She was doing this weird wee shuffley walk'
And I thought she was going to cry,
So I headed on over to talk to her,
(Cos I thought I might be in with a chance),
And I said "Is there anything I can do?"
And she said "No, I've shit in my pants!"

Well you know I never stress,
When there's a damsel in distress,
There's no problem can't be solved with clever thinking,
So I turned on all my charm,
And gently took her by the arm,
(But I didn't stand too close cos she was stinking!)

My plan was quick and easy,
And I hope you don't feel queasy,
I assure you that was never my design,
We just pulled up loads of grass,
With which to wipe her dirty ass,
And for knickers, I just let her borrow mine!

A Blank Canvas

Liquid pooh flew out my hole,
You know the type I mean,
It left me with a speckled bowl,
That took me hours to clean,
I flushed the loo and wiped the spots,
I made that toilet shine,
But first I played "Connect the Dots",
My finger drew the line!

I drew a star, a horse, a cart,
I've never drawn so well,
It really was a work of art,
(But a fucking awful smell!)
So next time diarrhoea strikes,
Don't let it get you down,
The Artist can draw whatever he likes,
But the colour must be brown!

Turnaround

If you're thinking that nobody likes you,
There's a chance that you might just be right,
You're maybe a horrible bastard,
Or you could be a miserable shite,
You might be plain nasty or smelly,
Or perhaps you're an arrogant prick,
And don't take affront,
But you might be a c#nt,
Or the sight of you makes people sick.

But it's only yourself who can change things,
As it's nobody's fault but your own,
If your life you embrace,
With a smile on your face,
There's a chance that you won't die alone!

And just one last word for those people,
Who bring laughter and joy to the sad,
Dial it back a wee bit,
We're all sick of your shit,
And it makes all us others look bad!

Pin Number Please?

I met my gorgeous girlfriend,
It was on the internet,
She sent me naked pictures,
Even though we'd never met.
I told her all about myself,
She said I'm cool and funny,
She tried to come and see me,
But she didn't have the money.

I volunteered to lend her some,
She sorted out the banking,
Then cleaned out all my bank accounts,
So now I'm back to wanking!

Dietary Advice

Every time I pick my nose,
I have to eat my snatters,
People always ask me why,
(They seem to think it matters!)
I'm not sure what it's all about,
It started in my teens,
I blame my mum, she used to shout
At me to "Eat my greens"

Wet Dream

I dreamt of bells the other night,
Big bells, all loud and swinging,
It's true, no joke,
Cos when I woke,
My bed was fucking wringing!

#Duh!

When you train to be a suicide bomber,
There's a part they forget to teach,
You might get all of those virgins,
But they'll only get a body part each!

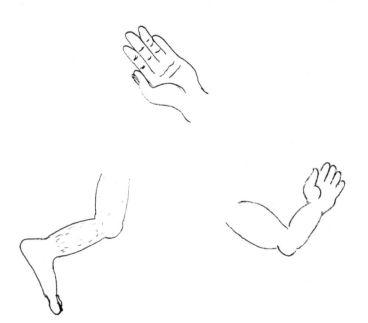

Step On It!

Growing older gracefully? well that's a friggin lie,
The stuff men have to go through is enough to make you cry,
But no-one seems to bitch or moan which I find kind of strange,
And that's the purpose of this poem cos that's about to change.

We always hear about the girls, the bloody menopause,
Vaginal dryness, Periods, (The "Keep your hands off" clause)
And Cellulite and Saggy Boobs or how their ass has grown,
But now it's time to fight back, we've got problems of our own!

When men hit 50 years of age, life gets a little tough,
Things go plop or drop or flop, it's rather nasty stuff,
We suffer from a problem and it isn't widely known,
We try to keep it secret and we think we're all alone,

I'm here to tell you don't despair,
Stop climbing up the walls!
It's just your age, you've reached the stage,
Of " OUL BOY SAGGY BALLS."

Now in case you haven't heard of it, just please let me explain,
It's quite a normal old age thing, there isn't any pain,
40 years of boxer shorts is bound to take its toll,
With no support, our balls distort, it's nature's birth control.

Step On It continued...

Don't get me wrong, it all still works, that's not quite what I mean,
It's just when someone gets a look, they end up not too keen!
(And it's also quite horrendous when you're sitting on the loo,
And your testicles are down below, astride a bit of pooh!)

So I know it has you worried and I don't wish to offend,
But I've done a bit of research and I'd like to recommend
An answer to the problem of your wrinkled dangly scrote,
A gift to all mankind, (within a poem that I wrote).

So do not fear, cos help is here, I've found a good solution,
The answer to our wayward balls, involving substitution.
Just throw away your boxer shorts,
Please give my plan a chance,
And gather up your goolies in a pair of UNDERPANTS!

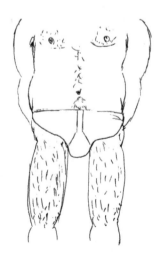

Helpful Hints

And

Advice

section.

Helpful Hint "Number 2"

When you're sitting on the toilet,
And your turd plops in the bowl,
Do you jump when "wee-wee" water,
Splashes up against your hole?

Just crumple up some toilet roll,
Then pooh on top of it,
And that'll stop the splash-back,
When you have to do a shit!

It's Not Penicillin !

If you eat bread,
That's coloured blue,
You'll end up dead,
Or on the loo!

Just Say No (or else OW!)

Don't do drugs,
It's really dumb,
The prison thugs,
Will hurt your bum!

Government Warning

Smokers die and that's a fact,
As smoking causes Cancer,
The odds against your life are stacked,
To quit's the only answer!

So throw away your cigarettes,
And all your bloody matches,
I promise you'll have no regrets,
Now go and buy some patches!

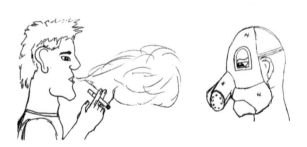

A Nasty Shock!

If toilet roll is not too strong,
Please wash your hands for twice as long!

Don't Use The Facecloth!

If diarrhoea burns your ring,
Apply some cream to ease the sting,
But first to wash away the stink,
Please rinse your bum-hole in the sink!

Misjudgement.

If your fart feels hot and wet,
Clean underpants you'll have to get!

You'll Pay Per View

Don't take your clothes off on the "Net"
Your friends and family won't forget!

If You Steal, You Squeal!

Little Johnny, naughty boy,
Went out shopping, stole a toy,
The Police came out, took him away,
And now in Jail he has to stay.

Now Boys and Girls, I'm sure you know,
That Jail is not the place to go,
Cos if you have to serve a term,
You'll end up full of cellmate sperm!

Aww for F's sake!

Please teach your kids to be polite,
In public toilets FLUSH YOUR SHITE!

Blowjob Request

If snot is dripping out your nose,
Please give it one or two big blows,
It's much politer I believe,
To use a tissue, not your sleeve!

Public Information Poem No. 1

Keith Totten's teeth were rotten,
Fifty shades of black,
The Dentist pulled them one by one,
(You should have heard them crack!)
He never flossed, He never brushed,
It was a fatal flaw,
And now poor Keith, without his teeth,
Sucks dinner through a straw.

So Girls and Boys, put down your toys,
And start this from today,
Always brush and floss your teeth,
To stamp out tooth decay.

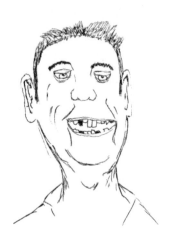

Public Information Poem No. 2

Suzy Sheen was just fifteen, her boyfriend was the same,
One night while talking on the phone, he asked if she was game
To send a picture of herself, I think you know the type,
Or better yet, he'd go online and watch her live on Skype.
He swore that no-one else would see,
And no-one else would know,
So silly Suzy went along and gave a private show.

Needless to say,
At School next day,
We know what happened next,
Suzy's private photographs
Were shared around by text.

Now luckily,
For our Suzy,
The Police came on the scene,
They tracked down every mobile phone,
And wiped their memories clean.
They talked to Suzy's boyfriend,
Their enquiries to assist,
And now each week he has to sign,
The Sex Offenders list!

Happy Ever After

Middle age has been and gone,
Prepare to lose all hope,
If life is like a mountain climb,
You're on the downward slope!

The nasal hair,
Is quite unfair,
The midnight pees are boring,
The extra weight,
Just isn't great,
And what about the snoring?

The passing gas,
(From out your ass),
Was once quite safe to do,
Advancing years,
Enhance your fears,
Of partial follow through.

The wrinkles deep,
The lack of sleep,
The creaky knees and back,
The dodgy gut,
The leaky butt,
Examining your sack!

Happy Ever After Continued …

But old age isn't all that bad,
Most people learn to cope,
There is no use in feeling sad,
Or trying to whinge and mope.

So please look back upon your life,
With love and tears and laughter,
You're not yet done,
Bring on the fun,
And Happy Ever After!

Last Words From Merv d' Perv Productions

I pick my nose, I scratch my bum,
I shave my pubic hair,
I don't like people riding bikes,
I wear girls' underwear,
My toilet roll, it must be tough,
(I like my fingers clean),
My girlfriend likes to trim her muff,
(My poems are obscene!)

I hope that you've enjoyed them all,
And found that some were funny,
And so it ends,
"Safe Home" my friends,
And thanks for all the money!

Glossary of terms

"Hoking" - Rummaging for – rhymes with joking!
"Snatters" - Irish slang for Nasal Mucus
"Fanny Pad" - Sanitary towel
"Oul doll" - Little old lady

DISCLAIMER

Any resemblance to real persons, living or dead, is not in some cases purely coincidental (You know who you are!).

All complaints about subject matter will be strictly ignored and in most cases laughed at and used without permission in future editions to ridicule the sender(s) of said complaints.

All grammatical errors are intentional and used for artistic and poetic effect.